The Charm Offensive

Darcy Delany

The Charm Offensive

Chapter One

When you think of a politician, you think of someone confident, aggressive and out for themselves.

I happen to be one of the exceptions, and—I hate to say—one of the flops.

Christian Lyons emits his melodic, deep laugh from across the lawn of the Senate courtyard. Dressed in a slim-fit blue suit that looks more hipster than politician, Christian Lyons is adored by the nation, according to his latest poll results.

An adulation I should have achieved.

My father was Prime Minister, as was my grandfather. The Hammonds are the Kennedys of Australia—well they were, until I took up the family business.

I continue glaring at Christian, who was unperturbed by this morning's parliamentary debate. I'd challenged him about taking a taxi to the Sydney Opera House and back one Saturday night, on the taxpayer dollar. No one supported me. I daresay they wanted to avoid similar scrutiny.

'You should have put the boot in him during question time, Nick. Your high-brow criticism wouldn't register with the public, let alone the opposition.'

Miranda Birch, my political adviser, has made Prime Ministers wince with her sharp observations and even sharper delivery. She's been my political adviser since last year, when my disastrous polling results were published. Dad recommended I find someone with experience in politics, rather than on Twitter.

'Miranda, I'm not getting into the gutter with Christian. I'll handle this my way.'

'Hmmph.' Miranda shakes her head, the strong scent of her hairspray wafting into my nose. 'The everyday person hates politicians who rort the system, Nick. Show them you don't stand for that and they'll notice.' One of Miranda's pencil-thin eyebrows quirks towards the evening sky.

'Miranda.' Yet another sycophant coming to pay homage to the great Miranda Birch. I nod at the man in the nondescript black suit—what is it with Canberrans and black?—and glance back at Christian, whose arm is slung behind his girlfriend's back. Caroline Brent could pick any man, but she chooses a slick politician like Christian. Well, if I'm cynical about it, she's using him to help her career; a political journalist survives on inside information and tips. It has nothing to do with his ready charm.

He laughs again, and I roll my eyes. It sounds so manufactured, and yet, as always, he holds his audience spellbound—including Caroline.

By the time I shift my gaze back, I'm alone with the dying essence of Miranda's hairspray, beer bottle in hand. I've become a social pariah since my poor poll results over the last few months.

My eyes travel straight to Caroline's peachy-skinned cheek, framed by honey-blonde hair which hangs in waves to her waist. She has the delicate features of a bird, but it's a false impression many politicians have underestimated, to their detriment. As one of Canberra's top political journalists, Caroline Brent hides a back bone of steel beneath that vulnerable façade. A shame she isn't more discerning with men, I think, taking a swig of beer.

Where there is smoke, there is fire, my father always says. He'd have looked for more dirt on Christian, then swooped in to win Caroline.

And that is my problem. I don't have what it takes to be a good politician.

Caroline Brent's keen journalistic ear recognises there is nothing worth paying attention to in this AFL discussion. Talk of salary caps, drafts and the technicalities of the game were things Christian didn't expect her to take part in.

'Caroline, just sorting out some business.' Christian places an absent-minded peck on her cheek before veering to a corner of the courtyard with his companion, the local developer opening the first aged-care estate in Australia. It would, in Christian's words, be a 'gated geriatric community', a title that made Caroline wince. Christian did not consider he would be 'geriatric' himself, one day.

But Caroline does. Often. Her own father died young, leaving

her mother to raise her and her siblings alone. Laughter and magic seemed to die in their home with her father, as her mother struggled with the demands of working and raising a family. From a young age she'd promised herself that she wouldn't struggle alone. She planned on having a large, happy family—when Christian proposed.

'We'll get engaged when I'm party leader,' he joked when they passed a jewellery store.

Caroline sighs. Christian's career was moving in that direction, but if she was to have the three children she'd always dreamed of, she needed to have them soon.

Gentle laughter and the clinking of glasses carries through the warm evening air, and she took a deep breath. Everything will turn out for the best—so her father used to say.

A darting movement in the far corner catches her eye. Nick Hammond, one hand holding a beer bottle, two fingers of the other hand pinching something small and dark between them. A frown furrows his brow as he bends down and places the item on the grass.

'What is it?' she mutters as she squints through a stray ray of sunshine.

'It's a snail.' Christian places his hand in the small of her back.

Normally Caroline objected to Christian touching her like that in public, but today, she smiles.

A grown man saving a snail?

She hasn't seen a man do something like that since—well, since her father was alive. She bites her lip as unbidden tears poke at the corners of her eyes. Despite the intervening years, her father has made himself felt at odd moments: a birthday; Father's Day and now, as Nick Hammond saves this tiny creature.

'A softy intellectual like Nick Hammond will never make it in politics.'

Caroline's cheeks flush warm, and she turns her face to Christian's. 'Why can't a politician be kind *and* successful?'

'Because politics is dirty. You know that.'

Caroline searches the dark blue of his eyes, which

flicker with the choppiness of a deep ocean trench. 'Why so philosophical?'

She shrugs. 'Bit of fun.' She knows her own brown eyes shimmer with emotion, something she only ever allows herself to do when she is 'off duty'. 'It's possible, don't you think?' She watches as Nick leaves the courtyard.

'Yeah, maybe in one of your movies.' A boyish grin spreads across Christian's face. So, he hadn't forgotten their movie night. It wasn't the most romantic date, but between her coverage of breaking news events and Christian's political duties, simple dates were the best they could manage.

She shivers as a blossom-scented breeze caresses her arms.

'Here.' Christian slides his jacket off his shoulders in a practised move and settles it around her own. His eyes catch hers, and one quirks into a wink. 'There. Jamie Fraser would be proud of me.'

Caroline's mouth eases into a smile, and she winks back. He has done well to remember her favourite movie hero, a man who would probably save a snail like Nick Hammond just had.

Would Christian?

Unlikely. A snail couldn't do anything for him in return.

Chapter Two

'20% preferred Candidate for ACT Senate.'

Miranda's sharp eyes glint at me over her newspaper.

'Well, it could be worse.' I give her a lopsided grin, and hope that I sound convincing. I dare not ask what Christian Lyon's ratings are.

'Hmmph. And I could be married to David Beckham.' Miranda lowers the paper and tilts her head to sip the last of her espresso, the smell reminding me of my own cooling coffee on the desk in front of me. I now associate coffee with bad news, since Miranda tells me the poll results as I sip my first cup each morning. I push the mug aside and take the paper, my stomach lurching as I read the headline: 'Harried Hammond: every dynasty has to end.'

'So what, I've had a few poor polls. Everyone has.' Right beside it is an article about political golden boy Christian Lyons: 'The rise and rise of the boy from the west,' the headline screams. It's made worse by the photo of a smug Christian standing with his arm around Caroline. If I was holding Caroline that way I'd look smug, too.

Miranda leans back in her chair.

'You're lucky the oldies love you. "A man of old-fashioned integrity".'

She fixes me with a gimlet eye, the same one that reduced a former staffer to confess she'd been leaking policies to the press.

'But if these results don't improve …'

There is nowhere to hide from Miranda, which is why I agreed to work with her. I knew she wouldn't treat me like the son of the former Prime Minister, but as a politician in my own right.

'Well, I'm not lowering my standards. I won't perform like some actor on a stage, like Christian-bleedin'-Lyons.' I stab my finger at the picture of Christian beside the poll results.

Miranda purses her lips and glances at the ground.

'What?'

Miranda might be inscrutable, but I've been watching people's mannerisms my whole life—long enough to know when someone's holding something back.

Miranda meets my gaze. 'You have three months to turn the polls around, or you're gone.'

Chapter Three

Sitting in the French inspired dining room of my parents' home, I watch my father's face turn beetroot red.

'They want to dump a Hammond?'

My father is seldom angry, but when he is, everyone around him stills, waiting for the eruption, hoping it might not happen. He stalks towards the window and rests his hand on the frame of the French doors.

'Darling, let's keep this in perspective.' Mum takes a sip of wine and gives me a small nod. Not even my father's anger perturbs my mother's serenity. 'It's a shot across the bow. A test. They want to see how Nick responds.'

My father's right eyebrow rises. The light has gone on, just as my mother intended.

'Hmm. They're goading him into showing some "bif", as they say.'

'Might help you in the romance department. Women love a man who exudes control.' My sister always steers the conversation back to my love life, or lack of one.

'Emmanuelle, pass the coffee, please.' Mum asks.

'Mum, I worry that I'm in trouble when you call me that. Just call me Em; everyone else does.'

My mother takes the *cafetière*. 'Darling, I did not give you a beautiful name only to shorten it. Your name defines you. Besides, I'm not everyone else, I'm your mother.'

Nice one, Mum, I think, as my sister and mother become engrossed in a discussion about the increasing casualness on society. Mum has a way of drawing conversations down unexpected but intriguing paths, and she knows Em can't resist a debate. Em might be younger than me, but she has a maternal desire to see me settled. And with the energy of a match maker on commission, she fixes me up with friends, friends of friends and even women she meets while shopping. But so far, no one has been right.

If they were more like Caroline Brent, though, perhaps they'd have a chance.

Dad's eyes narrow while he stares at Mum's pride and joy, the manicured foliage of her latest courtyard garden bed.

'I'm not lowering my standards to keep the press happy, Dad. I became a politician to make a difference.'

Dad turns and fixes me with a level look. 'But you can't make a difference if you aren't in power, can you?'

Mother clears her throat.

'It has to be said. He has a responsibility.'

Em, 'Yeah, to the peo …'

'To his family.' Father glares at me. 'Sort it out.'

Mum clears her throat again, louder this time.

'Flies and honey, remember, darling.'

Dad sighs as he surveys Mum's face. I've never seen anyone bring him to ground quicker than my Mum. She's like a modern-day Grace Kelly, the way she calmly brings him to heel without even raising her voice.

Dad walks over to Mum and kisses her on the top of her head. 'Look, son, just don't think about it so much, and you'll get an idea.'

Don't think about it so much. Hard not to when Mum and Em force me to sit through *Gone with the Wind*. Dad's fallen asleep; but given his penchant for interrupting every two minutes, Mum hasn't woken him.

Lucky him.

It's been a family tradition, watching an old movie together after our weekly family dinner. Soppy, I know, but it's better than spending time in my own sterile house, where the smell of paint hangs in the air, and the only piece of furniture is a sixties-style sofa I'd taken from Mum and Dad's. The right size to sleep on if I was in trouble with my future missus.

I will have a wife one day, but when? Friends from school married and settled down in their twenties, but I only seem to attract gold diggers or fame hunters.

My mind turns to Caroline. She's not flamboyant like Scarlett, but they do share a quiet steeliness I've always admired.

I stare at the screen as Rhett sweeps Scarlett into his arms, despite her protestations. It's pure fiction, but I have to admire his tenacity. Scarlett tells him she'll never say 'I love you' to him, but he presses on to win her anyway.

Wonder what he'd do if a political party wanted to dump him?

Probably give that sardonic smile and say 'I'd like to see them try.'

My mouth curls up into a grin.

Maybe this movie isn't such a waste of time.

Men grunt if you interrupt them during sports, but talk throughout your movies.

'Would you date a ranga, then?' Christian asks. It was his third stupid comment in as many minutes.

'I've not thought about it.' Caroline takes another bite of duck in plum sauce. *Too bad if he's bored, tonight was my turn to choose the movie. Besides,* aren't *Jamie Fraser's antics enough to keep a man interested?*

'She's a pain, that Claire. I'd have left her to the English.'

Caroline's mouth tingles as the sweet sauce settled on her tongue. 'Jamie will do anything for the woman he loves. That's why women love him.' *There. That should give him something to think about.*

'Hmmph. He's soft. And look what happens, his wife turns his life upside down! He lost his house because of her.'

'Love does that to a man, I suppose.' Caroline shrugs.

'Yeah, well, heaven help any man stupid enough to fall for a woman that hard.'

Christian rises from the sofa and pads to the kitchen, the light from the fridge spilling out over the tiled floor, bottles clinking as he removes another beer.

'Just going to the bathroom, keep watching.'

Just going to the bathroom. I know what he does in there, and where he gets it from. Her hand shakes, and she rests her glass on the coffee table. *Just make an excuse and leave early. Say you have a last-minute assignment. Better safe than sorry.* He'd grabbed her once, so hard he left bruises on her arms. He didn't even remember what he'd done, and when she confronted him, promised it would never happen again.

Her eye catches a flash coming from her right, where Christian had been sitting. A text.

Caroline glances back to the bathroom door. There is no shadow, suggesting he is still at the basin, snorting that garbage up his nose.

Her eyes fall on the phone once more. He never leaves his umbilical cord, as she calls it. He must have been desperate, not to notice he'd left it behind.

With a shaking hand, she reaches over and picks it up, finger hovering over the screen.

She swallows. Every instinct tells her to look, despite her now shaking body. She's honed those instincts over the years of her journalistic career. There is something there, something she needs to know.

With a gulp, she opens the message.

'The cat won't be squawking any more. Job sorted. Ten grand. Meet me tomorrow at the usual place.'

A shiver creeps down Caroline's spine.

The only reason anyone pays that amount of money is to have someone silenced. And they're not talking about the animal variety of cat, that is clear.

After another glance at the door, she opens another message.

And another.

All talk of cats, and the house.

House?

Parliament House, perhaps?

And sugar.

She frowns. *Christian calls that rubbish he's snorting his candy. Maybe that's it.*

But that's not it, the sinking feeling in her stomach confirms that. Christian is doing something far worse than taking cocaine.

I have to get out of here.

She wipes the phone on her skirt to remove her fingerprints, and puts it back where he'd left it, squashed beside the sofa cushion.

'Chris, I have to go. Something's come up.' She grabs her unopened overnight bag from the hall. 'Call you later.'

Christian coughs. 'Yep, right love.'

With her bag banging on her hip, Caroline dashes for the lift, heart pounding.

Chapter Four

'You're looking happy for someone whose head is on the block.' Miranda places my coffee on the desk and eases into her chair. The smell of coffee and the sight of my office desk no longer fills me with a sense of dread. I'm a man on a mission, and I'll need all the coffee I can get.

'I have a plan.' Christian Lyons and the rest baying for my political blood will be no match for a Rhett Butler.

'Do tell.' Miranda curves an eyebrow to the ceiling and leans back against the chair.

'It's called The Charm Offensive. And in essence, it involves me channelling Rhett Butler to keep my seat.' And maybe, win me Caroline.

Silence. Miranda winces. 'And how will that help your career?' She swallows, an indication of how hard she is working not to spit out 'are you f***ing serious?' or something similar.

I jump out of my seat and grab a whiteboard pen.

'Rhett Butler fascinated people because of his confidence and charisma. So no matter whether he was doing good things or bad things, he had power. Right?'

I turn to Miranda after jotting down 'Rhett-charisma-power' on the whiteboard.

'Go on.' She swallows once more. Not convinced yet, then.

'So what is it about Rhett that makes people, even those who dislike him, still respect him?

Miranda shrugs one shoulder.

'He oozes confidence and power through his dress and demeanour.

Miranda glances at my standard-issue navy blue suit.

'And he smiles like the cat who has the cream, so people wonder what he knows. And that throws them off balance, leaving him in a position of—that's right—power.

Miranda gives a small smile. She's enjoying this, then.

'He takes risks. People respect someone who flirts with danger.

I add "risks" to my list.

'And, he responds with witty lines a la Winston Churchill. It shows he's a thinker, but not above getting his hands dirty when needed.'

'He can shoot, too.' Miranda adds, nodding to the board.

I stop, whiteboard pen in the air. 'Good point. It's not popular, but then, neither am I.' Miranda's mouth falls open as I write the word 'shooting' on the board.

It's closed by the time I turn to her with a nod. 'So, what do you think?'

Miranda purses her lips and scans the board.

'Selling yourself to the public *is* the same as selling a story, I guess.' She sits down and crosses her arms.

'And not even Christian Lyons can match Rhett Butler.'

A slow smile spreads across Miranda's face. 'True. So, let's get started.'

Chapter Five

'Nick, this is Savina.'

Savina Sundie, the stylist of choice for Australia's most powerful people. I can only imagine what deals Miranda has done to have Savina standing here. I try not to squint at her bright orange dress. 'It's wonderful to meet you, Savina.' Her bracelets tinkle as she gives my hand a firm shake. Even her perfume, a combination of sunshine and citrus, is energising. If there's anyone who can help me pull this plan off, it's this woman.

'And you.' Savina's mouth spreads into a grin. 'When Miranda told me about The Charm Offensive, I had to be involved.' She leans towards me. 'I'm a *Gone with the Wind fan*, too.' She winks.

'I've done a storyboard of looks I wanted to show you.' I usher her to the leather settee and she places a flip-chart on the glass coffee table.

Miranda perches beside Savina, and I take the seat opposite.

'We need to balance Rhett's look with a style Australians will relate to. If you're too dressed-up, the public won't see you as "one of them".'

Savina flips open the folder, glossy nails tapping the tabletop.

'So we still go with suits, but you lose the tie. Shows that you are serious about your role, but aren't stuffy. We want to convey an element of rebelliousness.'

Rebelliousness? I can't help smirking.

'Something funny?' Savina arches her perfectly manicured left eyebrow.

'No, not at all.' I shake my head. 'Not much of a rebellion, though, is it? Not wearing a tie?'

'Well, you're a Hammond. If you copied James Dean, people wouldn't buy it.'

The front of my throat tightens. *Thanks. I already know I'm no James Dean.*

'Moving on,' Miranda says. I give her a wink for rescuing me, and I'm surprised when she winks back. Usually she'd make an acerbic comment about the inappropriateness of winking in today's politically-correct workplace.

'And stop shaving each day. Stubble appeals to women and men.' Savina winks, and Miranda, strike me down, giggles.

Now it's my turn to raise an eyebrow. Miranda Birch is enjoying herself?

'We also do a photo shoot of you at home. We'll bring in a stager to decorate it in my "James Bond's club" style. Dark woods, earthy colours, lots of smoked glass.' I glance at the picture of a library on the current page Savina is pointing at. Palms, wooden leather-topped desk and a fireplace in the background. It does resemble a study James Bond would have – and not in a good way.

'Isn't it a little . . . gaudy?'

Savina raises an eyebrow. 'This style is back in fashion, I'll have you know. Besides, doesn't every man want this sort of James Bond room? When men see it, they'll want to be you. And when women see it, they'll want to be with you.'

I glance back at the picture. James Bond is as far from me as Mars. I let out a sigh. Dad never had to work this hard and here I am, acting like someone I'm not for votes.

It's pathetic.

'I can't be someone I'm not. It's disingenuous. And I'm not disingenuous.'

Savina leans forward, the steeliness in her mocha-brown eyes softening. 'Nick, it's normal to feel awkward. But really, you're just becoming your true self.'

'Yeah, right.'

'No, *really*. This idea came from somewhere inside you. It's a sign a bolder you is ready to launch.'

'She's right.' Miranda nods 'Savina knows what she's doing, and so do I.' She fixes her gaze on me and folds her arms across her chest, daring me to disagree with her. 'Besides, your Dad trusted me to help you. And so should you.'

I glare back at Miranda. Of course she brings Dad into it. Like I need to be reminded I'm not the politician he was.

'No harm in giving it a try. Need to break a few eggs to make an omelette, don't you?'

Miranda smiles—a genuine smile, too. Gee, what is going on with her? 'Yes, you do. But enough with the clichés, please.'

Caroline doodles yet another star on her notebook, clenching her jaw. Normally she would enjoy watching Christian on the floor of Parliament, but today she wants to be as far away from him as possible.

'Mr Lyons wants to give an amnesty for drug-related crimes. I must say, I'm not surprised. It's the easy choice, and we all know our esteemed colleague has no backbone, the way he flops around whichever way the polls blow.'

The chamber erupts with howls of laughter, and a startled giggle escapes Caroline's lips.

Nick Hammond's appearances are usually lacklustre, but today, he commands the attention of everyone in the room. And it isn't just the new style. He's standing taller, with a gleam in his eye and a mischievous grin that makes her wonder what he's thinking. If he had a moustache, she imagines he'd be twirling it with pleasure. He is enjoying the theatre, something she never thought she'd see.

Or enjoy.

'I didn't realise Nick Hammond was so hot,' whispers a female journalist.

Caroline shrugs. The slim-fit indigo suit, no tie and a shadow of stubble across his jaw *is* attractive, she has to admit.

Christian jumps to his feet, arms waving, a grin on his face. He's enjoying the challenge. Like a street fighter, he always comes out swinging no matter what the odds against him. And he does it with confidence, the very quality that drew her to him. He only knows one way—up, or out. A man like that, one who has won battle after battle, was as close to invincible as she could find.

But he's not invincible, as it turns out.

A little pot now and then isn't a big deal, but cocaine?

She turns her gaze to Nick Hammond, whose dark eyes glisten with relish as he watches Christian speak. 'Is that all you've got?' his expression seems to say.

Caroline shakes her head and smiles, not caring who sees her. She doesn't know where this Nick

Hammond had been hiding, but she likes him. Far more than she wants to admit.

'Senator Lyons, why are you on this Committee? You don't care about young people trapped in the grasp of drugs, or those who love them.'

Christian gives a nonchalant wave before crossing his arms and laughing.

Nick continues. 'Well, I care about them. I want them to get their lives back, to live free of violence, fear and poverty. I want our doctors and nurses to do their work without the threat of being attacked.'

'Hear, hear,' Nick's colleagues yell.

Caroline's cheeks flush.

'I want to help people find the help they need before they turn to drugs. I ask you, Senator Lyons, do *you* care? Do *you* care enough to do what is right, rather than what is popular?' Nick raises his eyebrows at Christian, who grins back.

The gallery is silent.

'Well ladies and gentlemen, you have your answer.'

'Go Nick,' says the woman sitting beside her.

Caroline gives a small smile. She can't let her colleagues see her agreeing with Nick Hammond.

'Who would have thought Nick would be such a warrior?' the woman whispers again, eyes shining with admiration.

Who indeed.

Caroline watches as Nick resumes his seat with a smile, and her heart warms, the way it does when Jamie Fraser does something honourable.

Honourable. It isn't a word she can use about Christian anymore, is it?

'Oh, he's so swoon-worthy, isn't he?'

'Um—yes, I suppose.' Caroline continues staring at Nick.

All these years she thought Christian was a good man, and now, she realises, she doesn't truly know him.

What's worse, she has given her energy and love to someone whom she thought she could help. But she can't save someone involved in such evil.

She sniffs and fakes a sneeze, so people will think she is just suffering from hay fever. Everyone does in Canberra, after a while, with its dubious reputation for being the allergy capital of Australia.

Enough hesitating. I know I need to do something.

But what?

Caroline bites the corner of her lip.

She too will come under suspicion once Christian's activities are revealed.

Years of hard work damaged—and for what? A man who has lied to her.

Caroline glares at Christian, who whispers with one of his fellow ministers. He seems as carefree and cocky as usual, qualities she had at first admired in him. Now, she despises him for them. How can he act normal after what he's done?

She glances at Nick, who sits opposite Christian. They are opposites in other ways, too. Nick Hammond would never dream of misusing his position.

Nor would he betray a confidence.

If I tell him what has happened, he can have Christian dealt with quietly.

Caroline folds her arms across her chest. He is honourable to a fault. *Just the sort of man who can help me.*

Chapter Six

'It's working.' Miranda plops the newspaper on my desk, followed by three more.

Savina beams at me from the settee. '65% preferred candidate for ACT Senator.'

I skim through the headlines. 'Hammond hammers Lyons.'

'Hammond on fire.'

'The Hammonds are back!'

My chest tightens at the last one. 'We were never gone,' I mutter, letting the paper fall.

A knock comes at the door, and Henry, one of the mail officers, pops his head around the door. 'My two favourite ladies.'

I glance at Miranda. She usually chides Henry for entering without knocking, but today she is silent as he wheels in a trolley laden with envelope-filled crates. 'Another delivery for you, mate.' He takes one crate and places it on the floor. 'They've been screened. The things people send through the mail.' He grins at me and shakes his head before moving the second crate. 'Have fun sorting that lot out, Mrs Birch.'

Miranda smiles.

'Do you want chicken and noodles for lunch today?' Henry asks.

'Yes, thank you. Now unless you want to open and file *all* these envelopes, get moving.'

Henry blows Miranda a theatrical kiss and closes the door behind him.

'What was that?' I cross my arms over my chest, the way Miranda does when she's questioning me.

'Oh, it's this Charm Offensive of yours, it's catching! Everyone's smiling, winking, dressing up.' Miranda permits herself to smile. Her eyes crease into lines that her expensive cream will have to work twice as hard to erase.

'You and Henry aren't ... 'I glance over at the vase of red roses towering in a crystal vase on the console.

'*What?*' Miranda gives a groan of disgust. 'He's young enough to be my son!'

Savina giggles.

'No, I'm not. Not that it's any of your business.' A pink hue creeps into her cheeks.

'Whoever he is, he agrees with you.' Today, instead of her head-to-toe black, she's wearing a deep purple shift dress, with low kitten heels. The purple lends a warmth to her skin and catches the violet tones of her blue eyes.

'Miranda, I didn't mean to upset you.' Hell, that's all I need now.

A knock comes at the door.

'Yes, Henry, I do want sweet chilli sauce,' Miranda calls out.

'Oh, sorry, were you expecting someone?' I jump as Caroline Brent peers around the door.

'Um, no … well, you see, Miranda thought you were …' I'm stammering, and I'm sure my cheeks are as red as Miranda's were.

'Caroline.' Miranda rises from the sofa and glides over to the door. 'We were going for a coffee, weren't we, Savina?' Miranda jerks her head at the door.

'Were we?' Savina stands.

'Yes. Now come on, I don't want to miss out on one of those new caramel slices.'

The door closes and I'm alone with Caroline. I'd like to pinch myself to be sure I'm not dreaming. My eyes travel down the delicate lines of her neck to the lacy pattern of her navy dress. She follows my eyes and gives a shy smile—a smile that says she likes me looking at her.

I swallow, and wave towards the settee, where Caroline takes a graceful seat.

My heart skips as she smiles that slow smile at me once more. Now I understand how Helen of Troy could launch a thousand ships.

But Caroline is a political journalist, and the girlfriend of my opponent. Not to mention that she's here just as my polling results improve. It's all too convenient.

I clear my throat. 'So, how can I help?'

Caroline's eyes crease gently. Confused? Concerned? Who can tell. I don't know her well enough to discern the difference, but I'm not stupid enough to assume she's here because she wants to see me.

'I take it this isn't a social call?' I sit taller in my chair and fold my hands across my knees in my 'I'm listening' gesture.

Her brown eyes scan my face as I try not to stare. She's more delicate this close, fine boned and small, with a mass of curly blonde hair cascading to her waist like a modern-day version of Rapunzel. Her perfume adds to the already heady mix of sensations, and I clench my jaw. *Focus.*

'I'm not sure how to tell you this.'

I nod, encouraging her to continue.

'I need to tell you something about Christian.'

She looks at the ground. 'I can't believe I'm doing this,' she says, half to herself, before shuddering.

'Caroline,' I lean forward, resisting the urge to touch her arm. She seems genuinely upset, and as much as I want to comfort her, I'm not going to let my guard down just yet.

She takes in a sharp breath as her eyes fill with

tears, and my resolve falters as I gave at her. 'He . . . takes drugs.'

And then I'm back to being a politician. Caroline always seemed so worldly to me, not one to be concerned about a casual joint. I manage to mouth an 'Okay' to be polite. But then her hands shake, and I suspect there is something more. I wait, my heart beating like a drum as the seconds pass.

'Cocaine, okay. Not some weed every now and then.'

I do frown, now. 'Really?' I think back to all the times I've seen him—not once has there been a hint of drug taking.

'He hides it well. But that's not why I'm here.' She inhales a deep breath. 'He gets the drugs from prisoners he's met through the Senate Committee you're both on.'

'Ah.' My eyebrow quirks up, but other than that, I give no other sign of my racing mind. This is political dynamite—but it's also a revelation that can destroy Caroline's career. Something she seems to understand well enough, judging by her shaking hands.

I want to reach out and take them in my own, and tell her everything will be okay. But first I need to be sure she's telling the truth.

'Sorry. I'm a mess.' Caroline looks at me, eyes

moist, and any defensiveness I have has melted away in the depths of her caramel eyes.

'No – you're fine,' I mumble. *Snap out of it Hammond. Stay on your guard.*

'Well,' Caroline clears her throat. 'I came here to ask you something.' She lifts her chin. 'Will you help me? I don't know what to do.'

Chapter Seven

'Smile,' Savina whispers as she fixes my lapel.

My fake fireplace glows in my new study, which is filled with a polished walnut desk. Mum hovers in the background, murmuring approval at the furnishings and taking notes of rug colours and plant names. Em floats past the staging assistants, smiling effusively and chatting with what seems to be aimless intent. Little do they know her talent for extracting valuable information from such innocent interactions. ASIO had offered her a job, which she'd turned down, much to Dad's disappointment.

I mouth the words I'd written earlier, about standing for something, taking risks; yet I'm caught like a proverbial deer in the headlights when I'm presented with information that needs decisive action.

I called in a favour from an old investigator friend who said Caroline's information looks genuine.

Now I am sure she is telling the truth, I have a decision to make. Do I risk my own political career to do the right thing? Christian is popular, and has friends in the media, police and the judiciary. I've heard of cases with more evidence than this being buried, the guilty parties never paying for their crimes.

'That's all we need for today, Mr Hammond. We'll be in touch.' The photographer shakes my hand before Savina walks him to the front door, followed by the last of the staging assistants. As soon as it clicks shut after them, I groan and stand up from my desk.

'Damn, damn, damn!' I slam my hand onto the door jamb, sending a thud reverberating through the wall.

I go to the fridge hidden in the American walnut cabinet and take out a beer.

Damn living in a modern world. If I'd been alive when *Gone with the Wind* was set, I could call Christian Lyons out and be celebrated for it. Instead, I need evidence to convict him.

And Caroline wants to gather it. She is the only one with access. If I send someone in, he might get suspicious and delete everything.

It is our best option. Still, it feels wrong.

I thump the beer bottle onto the desk, sending the tumblers tinkling.

I need to talk to Dad.

My tight chest eases once I walk into Dad's study, with its picture-laden walls, sturdy wooden furniture and polished leather calms the senses. Inside its walls my father has weaved his magic as a statesman and a parent. No matter how busy he was when I was growing up, all I had to do was appear in his doorway and he'd welcome me in.

Nothing has changed.

Mum has warned him of my impending visit, and the whisky is already in the glasses when I arrive. I breathe in the familiar smell of orange oil and my cartwheeling stomach quietens a notch.

Whatever he thinks about my political performance, he is still my Dad.

'You believe she's telling the truth?'

'I've had her claims investigated. Christian is up to something.'

'We need to be more certain than that. She's dating a man who's trying to damage your career. She comes to you when you're polling well and gives you information with which to pillory her boyfriend, at risk to your own career.'

Dad takes a sip of his whisky, holding my gaze.

'Caroline's different.'

Dad's eyes glisten. 'Ah. Does she know?'

I shake my head. 'She wouldn't have come to me, otherwise.'

Dad leans back in his chair. 'I think that's exactly why she came to you.' He grins. 'Which makes the way forward very simple.'

Chapter Eight

'Hi, I didn't think you were coming over today?' Christian beams at Caroline, and her stomach knots.

Good. He isn't suspicious.

'I wanted to surprise you.'

She pads after him, holding her breath until they reach the white, glossy open-plan kitchen. Just being in the confined hallway is enough to make the blood pound in her ears.

'You've been working too hard.' Christian flicks on the kettle.

Caroline nods. The dark circles under her eyes from nights spent awake worrying about Christian are coming in useful. 'It's always busy when an election is looming.'

He walks over to her and put his hands on her shoulders, his eyes searching hers.

Caroline stiffens her back muscles, willing herself not to shudder.

'I'm glad you came over. I have an idea—why don't we visit some jewellery stores?'

Her stomach sinks to the polished wood floors. Fate has a funny sense of humour. *When things were going well, Christian laughed off talk of an engagement. Now, when it's the furthest thing from my mind, he wants to move ahead?*

Caroline's shoulders sag as her mind searches for a plausible excuse. She had been expecting to spend the day reading the papers and watching TV, not cementing their relationship. Besides, she has to get into his phone to gather evidence for Nick.

'Sweetheart,' she purrs, her stomach lurching at the word, 'I would love to, but I am too tired to enjoy it.' She winds her arms around his neck and ruffles her fingers through his hair. Christian's eyelids dip. It works every time when she wants to get him in the mood. 'We've waited so long. Would you mind waiting until the election is over? So I can *really* enjoy the experience? It's not every day you get engaged.'

Christian's jaw muscle twitches, and she holds her breath.

If I can just get him to sleep, then I can get what I need from his phone. Otherwise he gets away with it. She almost purses her lips, but remembers her act and forms them into what she hopes is an alluring pout instead. Right now she is no better than the politicians she attacks for their duplicitous behaviour. Well, except Nick. Her cheeks flush warm.

What would he be like in bed? She smiles.

Christian shakes his head and grins at her. 'I can never resist *that* look,' he says, holding her gaze. 'I know I'm not perfect, but I do love you.' His pupils dilate, and for a moment she can almost believe it's because he loves her. But it's probably because he has had a hit. A lump forms in her throat.

'I know,' she says, her voice husky. In his own way, he does love her. But love shouldn't threaten to destroy her and all she's worked for. Caroline gazes back at him with a heavy heart. He will never change if she confronts him. He'll just present a façade, like he does, she now realises, with everyone.

'Come on,' Christian says, taking her by the hand and leading her to the bedroom.

Caroline shivers. *I can't sleep with him. The only way out is to fake an illness and hope he leaves me alone.*

She gags. 'I'm going to be sick,' she splutters, before running past Christian to the bathroom.

Chapter Nine

'Nick, I still feel I'm being disloyal to Christian.' Caroline squints up at me through the early summer sun as we walk around Lake Burley Griffin. I watch a group of pushy lycra-clad cyclists veer between walkers and joggers ahead of us before replying. To think I expected a measure of solitude at 6 a.m.

I stop, and Caroline comes to a halt beside me. 'I understand, but you are doing the right thing.'

She looks out over the lake, her lips pursed. 'I knew you would. I'm sorry I woke you so early of bed. I'm not the type to call people at 5 a.m. . . .. Her voice cracks, and she looks up at me.

I peer down at Caroline's round-rimmed sunglasses. They're far too big on her and make her appear even frailer. And the way she looks up at me like that, so trusting, so small, sends every rational thought fleeing from my mind. The air is heavy with anticipation.

For a nanosecond I wonder if I should tell her, but I can't bear to see her hurt any more than she is. Besides, I rationalise, she'll only blame herself for the outcome.

Then Caroline scrunches her nose with those

ridiculous glasses—and I don't hesitate. I reach forward and touch the glasses, stilling a moment before lifting them.

Her breath catches in her chest with an audible gasp. In the next second I've lifted the glasses away and am looking into her eyes. She swallows.

Early morning joggers run past us, and I sense eyes on my back; hear whispers as they pass. But I don't care.

'We shouldn't.' She glances out of the corner of her eye, then back at me, before biting her lip. A soft lip, *sans* lipstick, but with a hint of peachy-pink in the early morning glow.

'Who cares,' I whisper. And right now, I don't care. Hang Christian, and anyone else for that matter. Instead, I wrap her in my arms, waiting to see whether she backs away.

But Caroline stands still, staring up at me.

So with interminable slowness to savour the moment, I lean forward and place the gentlest kiss on her soft lips.

And to my utter delight, Caroline kisses me back.

The tearoom of Caroline's newspaper office is the place where the real work is done, especially when cake is involved. But today she hopes that her secret will remain just that, rather than become fodder for a game of political intrigue. A naïve hope, perhaps, but then Nick Hammond is the sort of man who makes a woman believe in the impossible.

I did the right thing, telling Nick. You can tell so much from a person's kiss, she thinks with a smile.

'Are you okay? You're flushed.'

Prue. She sniffs out stories like a bloodhound, and the way she looks at her now, she suspects something.

'Must be that virus everyone's been sick with lately.'

Prue narrows her eyes a smidge, just at the edges. She doesn't believe it. 'Must be.'

Caroline turns to focus on a throng of people coming into the tearoom. Journalists are like bloodhounds when it comes to cakes, too.

'Shut up, something's happening.'

The accountant reaches up a tattooed arm and increases the volume on the television.

Nick's face appears on the screen, brow knotted in a frown.

Caroline's breath catches in her chest. *There's nothing newsworthy happening on the Hill today. Unless...*

No, he wouldn't.

'I have a duty to you all, and to the public, to share some disturbing information I have referred to the Australian Federal Police.'

Oh no. No!

'I have reason to suspect that Senator Lyons has a connection to the disappearance of a prison warden from the Andrew Maconochie centre.'

A collective gasp bounces off the walls, and all eyes swivel in Caroline's direction.

No. This isn't happening.

The blood rushes to her head, and Caroline pushes through the crowd.

'Caroline, are you alright?' Nick holds an oversized bunch of red roses in his hand. They are wrapped in layers of red and white tissue paper, and curled ribbon hangs in festoons over his hand. He glances down the silent hall outside her apartment, which is, for once, void of its usual throng of traffic.

Under any other circumstances, she would be touched at the effort, but her chest heaves. 'Alright? Of course I'm not alright. What the hell were you doing?'

'The right thing.' Nick frowns. 'I couldn't tell you this before, but . . . he glances to his left and right. 'May I come in? This isn't a conversation for a hallway. Even an empty one.'

Caroline steps back, arms crossed over her chest, and glares at Nick until the door closes behind him.

'You were saying?'

'After you gave us what you had, we found out that Christian was involved in a drug smuggling operation into Sydney.'

'Smuggling?' She whispers.

Nick nods. 'I know I could have just left it to the police to deal with. But to be honest, I wasn't sure I could trust it to come to light if I did. Christian is very popular.'

Caroline searches his eyes. Nothing there but sincerity, and sadness.

'I hate that you heard about it the way you did. But I figured that if you were shocked, people would think you had no idea what was going on, and that would make it easier for you, professionally.'

'Oh.' Caroline's cheeks flush. 'I thought . . .' Her voice falters.

'That I was out to score political points?' Nick shakes his head. 'I don't blame you. I would too.'

Caroline gulps down the tears that well up in her throat. He had tried to protect her, not use her. And he'd come straight from Parliament to check on her- with flowers. Christian had only bought her flowers once, on their one-year anniversary. Never after an argument; she'd been lucky to hear him say 'sorry'.

'I'll leave. I don't want to upset you anymore.'

'No!' Caroline hears herself say. 'I mean', she swallows. 'It would be nice to have someone to talk to. Coffee?'

Nick beams. 'Lovely.'

They walk down the corridor amidst a rustling of tissue, the air heavy with anticipation. She can feel Nick's eyes on her, and her mouth waters as they reach the kitchen.

Her chest pounds as she turns to him and reaches out for the bouquet. 'Let me put them in some water.'

Their fingertips brush, and she gulps, before raising her eyes to his.

In a deft movement he places the flowers in the sink, and wraps his arms around her waist, his cologne—woody, masculine, traditional—causing resistance to fade with each breath.

'I love you, Caroline.' His voice is soft and low, his eyes locked on hers.

Caroline peers at him, heart thudding, as the words she'd so longed to hear ring in her ears. *Did he really say it? Or am I imagining it, because I want it to be true?*

Her hand reaches up and touches his heart, searching for any hint that he is lying. She wants so much to believe she is being rescued by a knight in shining armour, one whose chest rises and falls beneath her shaking hand.

'I love you,' he repeats, his mouth broadening into a grin

This time there is no mistake.

Caroline's chest rises with a sharp intake of breath, her mouth unable to form the words she wants to say in reply. And as his lips touch hers, she knows that she doesn't have to.

Chapter Ten

As the sun beams onto the dove grey walls of my lounge room, it catches on the rose gold vase filled with white hydrangeas and pink camellias. The room is graced with flowers now, but two plastic palms serve as a remnant of my bachelor days.

The serious-faced journalist adjusts her tortoiseshell glasses on her nose, and I stifle a laugh. Caroline has that same mannerism. I wonder what the journalist would say if I told her that? She glances at me, grins, then looks away.

Great. I must be doing my 'cat that has the cream' smile a la Rhett Butler again. Funny how something you practice becomes an ingrained habit.

'Senator, you established the Clear Path Foundation to help vulnerable people find help rather than turning to drugs. How does it feel to have countries such as the United States and United Kingdom running pilots of the program?'

'I'm thrilled. Thrilled because I know the program the foundation runs works. 100,000 lives turned around in Australia alone since it began. 100,000 families saved the trauma of trying to save someone they love. If I left politics tomorrow, it would be my proudest achievement.'

The journalist's eyes widen. 'Are you considering a departure from politics?'

I laugh. 'No, sorry to disappoint anyone who's hoping to see the back of me.'

'Glad to hear it. We need more politicians with a sensitive side.' The journalist and Caroline exchange a look.

'I told her about the snail.'

'Snail?'

'Do you remember when you picked up the snail in the courtyard?'

I frown as I struggle to remember.

'It was when you were polling badly.'

And then it comes flooding back. Me standing alone in the courtyard, forlorn about my career and wondering how I'd ever win a woman like Caroline.

'You see, people think that politicians need to be harsh. But the truth is, they must have heart. My husband has so much love for people, and that's what makes him such a wonderful politician.'

She gazes up at me with such love that I struggle not to lose my composure.

I take Caroline's hand in mine, rubbing the place where her wedding ring used to be. To think we'll be parents in three months—I glance down at her belly and clench my jaw so I don't become teary. It's hard not to when I imagine how differently things might have turned out. If it hadn't been for The Charm Offensive . . .

'Mrs Hammond, the ladies of Australia will want to know—is being married to the Nick Hammond what you imagined it to be?'

Caroline beams, her cheeks glowing pink. 'It's like living in a modern-day fairy tale.' She squeezes my hand. 'One I hope never ends.'

The End

About the Author

Darcy Delany writes adult fiction and children's stories – most of which involve sassy, quirky or cheeky main characters.

Darcy is based in Canberra, Australia – a haven for writers, with winter temperatures that encourage hibernation with a good book or manuscript.

Darcy loves history, fabulous food and old movies.
You can connect with Darcy at
https://www.storieswithsass.com

Other Books by Darcy Delany

Love Gone Wrong:
Short stories about love and all its debacles

Sweet Revenge:
Sometimes Karma Needs a Little Help

I Don't Date in December:
The Modern Day Fairy Tale Series- Book One

The Go-Between:
The Modern Day Fairy Tale Series Book Two

A List-Less Life:
Women of Sass, Book One

www.ingramcontent.com/pod-product-compliance
Lightning Source LLC
Chambersburg PA
CBHW071217130626
46555CB00004B/1741